Aladdin
and the Wonderful Lamp

Alexis Roumanis

www.av2books.com

Your AV² Media Enhanced book gives you a fiction readalong online.
Log on to www.av2books.com and enter the unique book code from
this page to use your readalong.

AV² Readalong Navigation

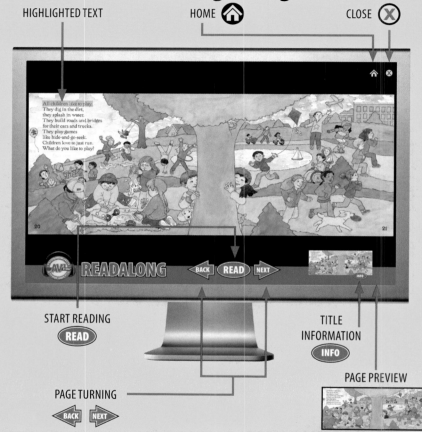

HIGHLIGHTED TEXT　　　　HOME 🏠　　　　CLOSE ❌

START READING
READ

PAGE TURNING
BACK **NEXT**

TITLE
INFORMATION
INFO

PAGE PREVIEW

Go to **www.av2books.com**,
and enter this book's
unique code.

BOOK CODE

| Y678459 |

AV² by Weigl brings you media
enhanced books that support
active learning.

Published by AV² by Weigl
350 5ᵗʰ Avenue, 59ᵗʰ Floor New York, NY 10118
Websites: www.av2books.com

Printed in the United States of America in Brainerd, Minnesota
1 2 3 4 5 6 7 8 9 0 20 19 18 17 16

032016
012915

Library of Congress Control Number: 2016930572

ISBN 978-1-4896-5230-0 (Hardcover)
ISBN 978-1-4896-5232-4 (Multi-user eBook)

Copyright ©2008 by Kyowon Co., Ltd.
First published in 2008 by Kyowon Co., Ltd.

There once was a boy named Aladdin.

One day, he met a strange man in the street.

"Aladdin, I am your uncle," said the man.

"I did not know I had any uncles,"
replied Aladdin.

"Can you take me to your
house?" asked the man.

Aladdin agreed, and took the man
to his home.

"I didn't know my husband had a brother," said Aladdin's mother upon meeting the stranger.

"I have been traveling for years," replied the man. "Where is my brother?"

"He died when Aladdin was very little," she said sadly.

The man embraced Aladdin and said, "I want to help you."

"How?" exclaimed Aladdin.

"Come with me. I will help you become as rich as I am," he replied.

Aladdin's mother agreed to let Aladdin go with his uncle.

Aladdin's uncle took him into
the mountains and built a fire.

"You must help me by doing a
magical dance," said his uncle.

His uncle took some powder from a small pouch
and threw it into the air.

"I command the ground
to open," he chanted.

"Now stomp the ground, Aladdin," he cried.
Aladdin stomped his feet.

There was a loud crack, and the ground opened.
A long staircase led deep into the earth.

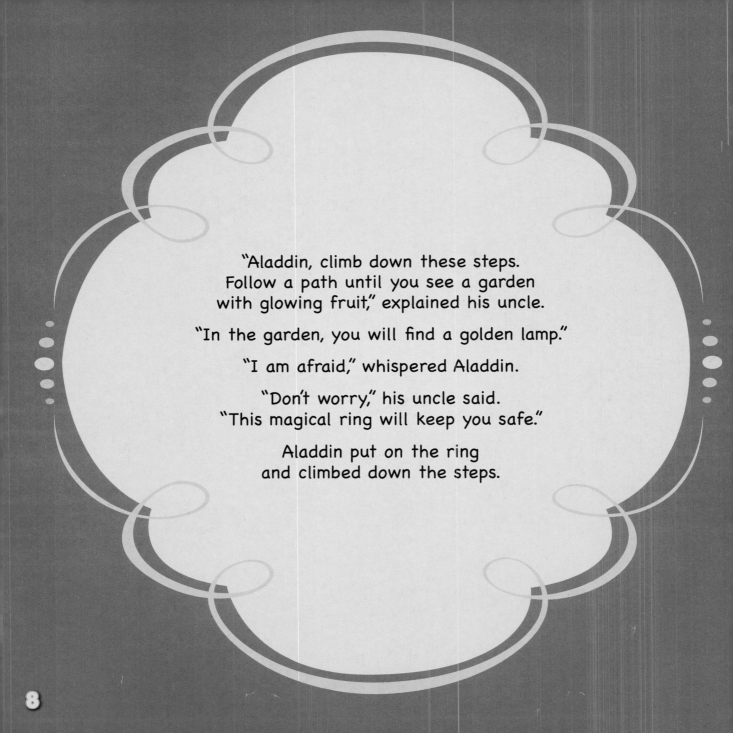

"Aladdin, climb down these steps.
Follow a path until you see a garden
with glowing fruit," explained his uncle.

"In the garden, you will find a golden lamp."

"I am afraid," whispered Aladdin.

"Don't worry," his uncle said.
"This magical ring will keep you safe."

Aladdin put on the ring
and climbed down the steps.

When Aladdin reached the garden, he saw
a golden lamp hanging from a rope.

He climbed a ladder and unhooked the
lamp from the rope.

Aladdin took a closer look at
the glowing fruit.

"Those aren't fruit!" he cried.
"They're gems!"

He quickly filled his pockets with gems,
and headed back up the stairs
to his uncle.

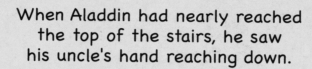

When Aladdin had nearly reached
the top of the stairs, he saw
his uncle's hand reaching down.

"Give me the lamp," he demanded.

"Why don't you wait until I get
out of here?" asked Aladdin.

"Be quiet, boy!" shouted his uncle. "Pass me the lamp."

"I won't give you the lamp until I am out
of this hole," Aladdin replied firmly.

"I will return when you have learned
your lesson!" yelled his uncle.

With a magical spell,
he made the hole in the ground
close up. Aladdin was trapped below.

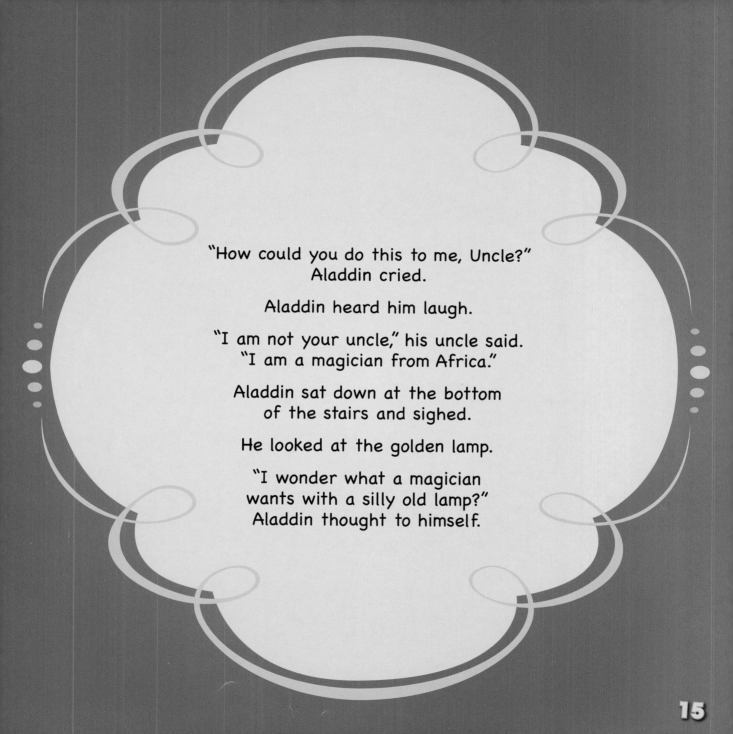

"How could you do this to me, Uncle?"
Aladdin cried.

Aladdin heard him laugh.

"I am not your uncle," his uncle said.
"I am a magician from Africa."

Aladdin sat down at the bottom
of the stairs and sighed.

He looked at the golden lamp.

"I wonder what a magician
wants with a silly old lamp?"
Aladdin thought to himself.

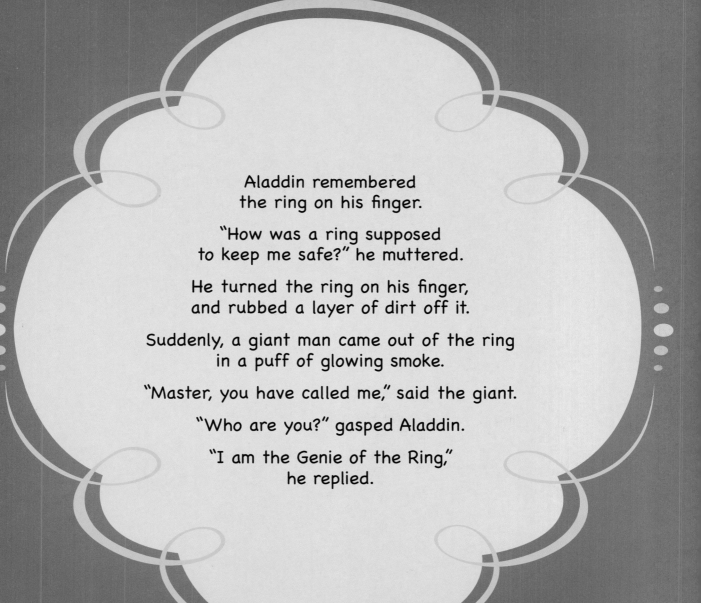

Aladdin remembered
the ring on his finger.

"How was a ring supposed
to keep me safe?" he muttered.

He turned the ring on his finger,
and rubbed a layer of dirt off it.

Suddenly, a giant man came out of the ring
in a puff of glowing smoke.

"Master, you have called me," said the giant.

"Who are you?" gasped Aladdin.

"I am the Genie of the Ring,"
he replied.

"What is a genie?" asked Aladdin.

"I can make any wish come true,"
the genie boomed in reply.

"Can you take me home?" asked Aladdin hopefully.

"Of course, Master," said the genie.

He opened the entrance,
and flew Aladdin back to his house.

"Remember to rub the ring anytime you need
my help," the genie added. Then,
he disappeared in a puff of smoke.

Aladdin told his mother
everything that had happened.

"Why would he want a dirty old lamp?"
she wondered.

She began to clean the lamp with a cloth.

"Oh my!" she cried, as a genie
shot out of the lamp.

Aladdin saw that this was not the genie
that he had met earlier.

"I am known as the Genie of the Lamp,"
the man said.

"What can I do for you, Master?"

Aladdin's mother was frightened,
but Aladdin had an idea.

"Can you bring us food to eat?" asked Aladdin.

"Your wish is my command,"
responded the genie.

He returned in a flash with
two large trays of food.

"Rub the lamp anytime you need my help,"
said the genie. Then, he disappeared.

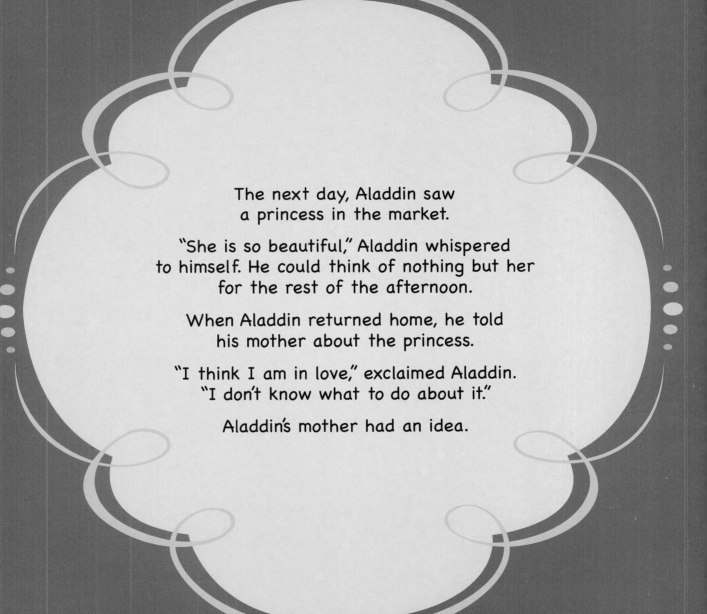

The next day, Aladdin saw
a princess in the market.

"She is so beautiful," Aladdin whispered
to himself. He could think of nothing but her
for the rest of the afternoon.

When Aladdin returned home, he told
his mother about the princess.

"I think I am in love," exclaimed Aladdin.
"I don't know what to do about it."

Aladdin's mother had an idea.

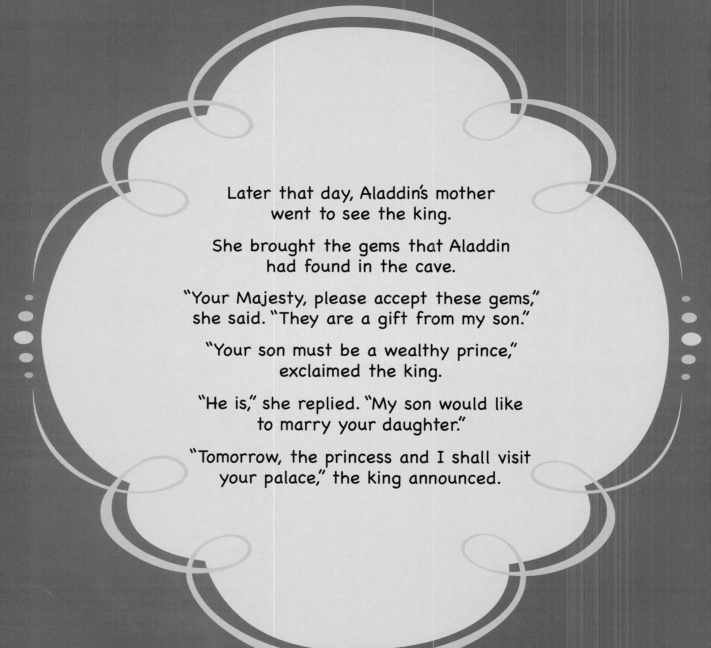

Later that day, Aladdin's mother
went to see the king.

She brought the gems that Aladdin
had found in the cave.

"Your Majesty, please accept these gems,"
she said. "They are a gift from my son."

"Your son must be a wealthy prince,"
exclaimed the king.

"He is," she replied. "My son would like
to marry your daughter."

"Tomorrow, the princess and I shall visit
your palace," the king announced.

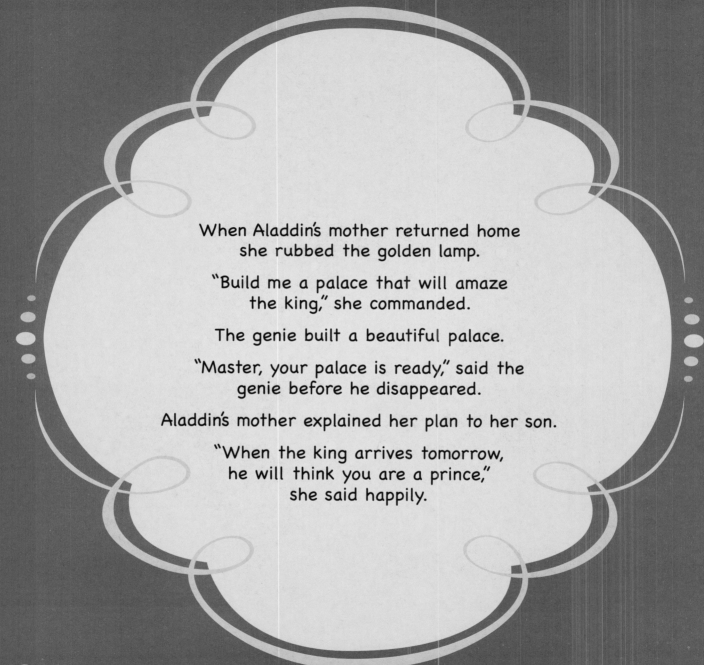

When Aladdin's mother returned home
she rubbed the golden lamp.

"Build me a palace that will amaze
the king," she commanded.

The genie built a beautiful palace.

"Master, your palace is ready," said the
genie before he disappeared.

Aladdin's mother explained her plan to her son.

"When the king arrives tomorrow,
he will think you are a prince,"
she said happily.

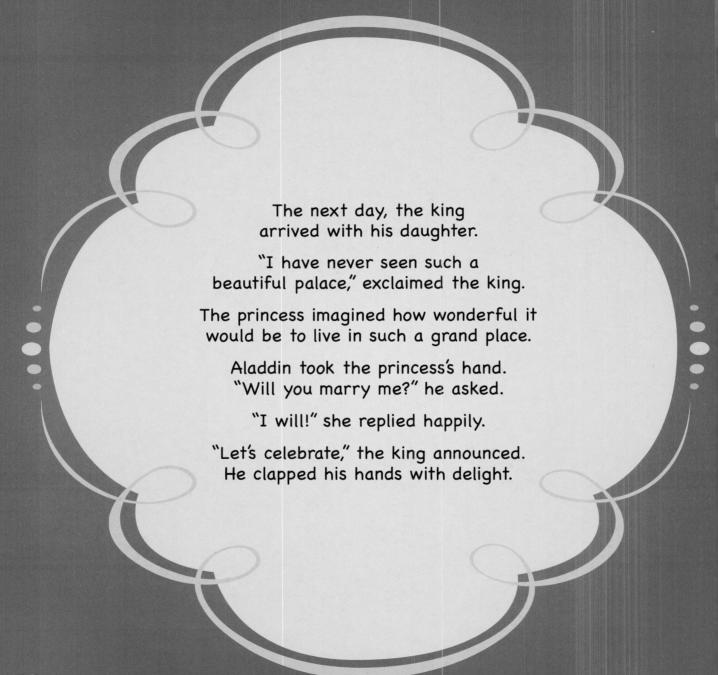

The next day, the king
arrived with his daughter.

"I have never seen such a
beautiful palace," exclaimed the king.

The princess imagined how wonderful it
would be to live in such a grand place.

Aladdin took the princess's hand.
"Will you marry me?" he asked.

"I will!" she replied happily.

"Let's celebrate," the king announced.
He clapped his hands with delight.

When the magician heard about Aladdin's
good fortune, he decided to visit his palace.

He waited until Aladdin went to the market,
and entered carrying a basket of new lamps.

"I am here to replace your old lamps
with new ones," he told the princess.

"That is very kind of you," said the princess.
She gave him Aladdin's magical lamp.

The magician took it
and gave her a new lamp.

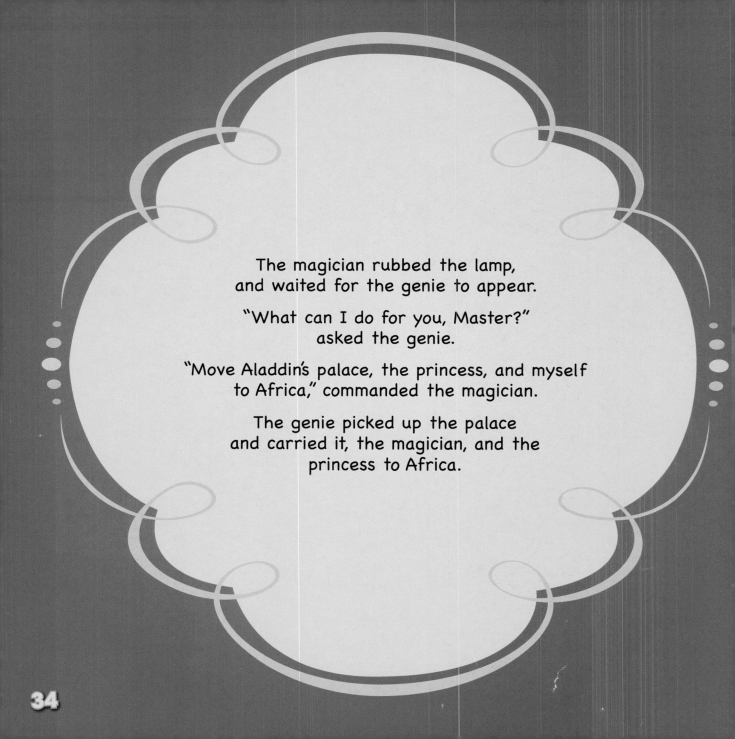

The magician rubbed the lamp,
and waited for the genie to appear.

"What can I do for you, Master?"
asked the genie.

"Move Aladdin's palace, the princess, and myself
to Africa," commanded the magician.

The genie picked up the palace
and carried it, the magician, and the
princess to Africa.

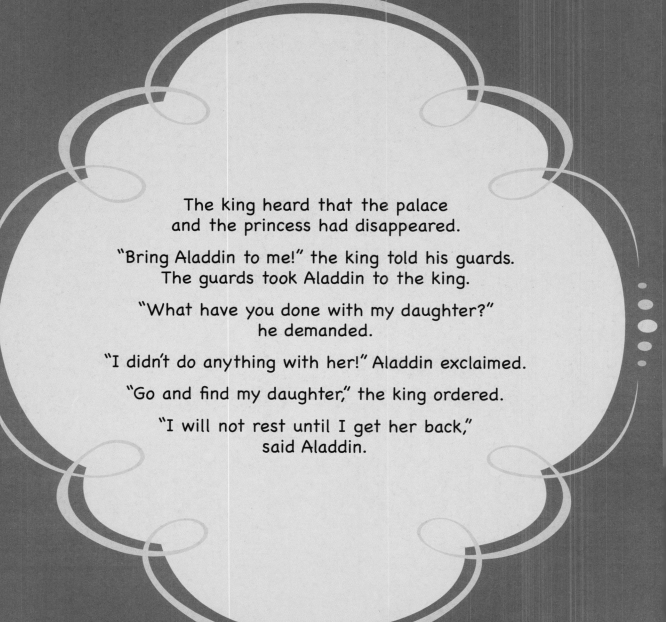

The king heard that the palace
and the princess had disappeared.

"Bring Aladdin to me!" the king told his guards.
The guards took Aladdin to the king.

"What have you done with my daughter?"
he demanded.

"I didn't do anything with her!" Aladdin exclaimed.

"Go and find my daughter," the king ordered.

"I will not rest until I get her back,"
said Aladdin.

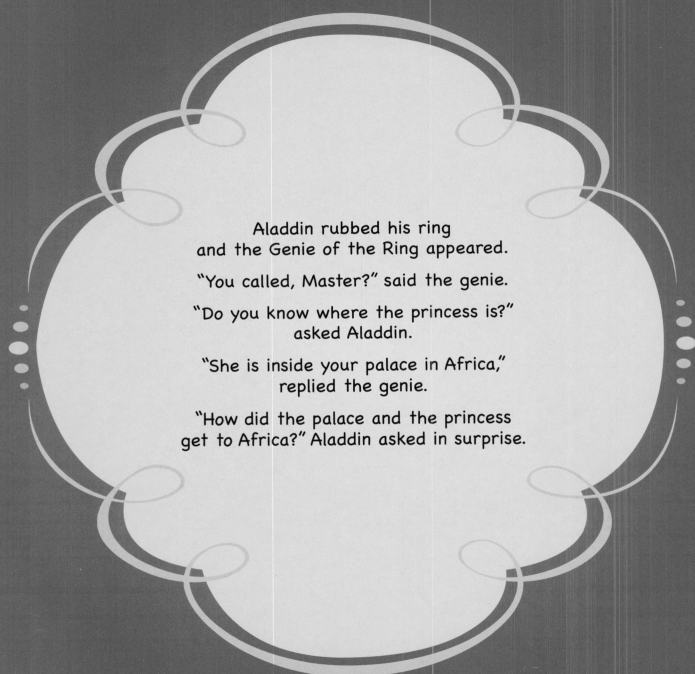

Aladdin rubbed his ring
and the Genie of the Ring appeared.

"You called, Master?" said the genie.

"Do you know where the princess is?"
asked Aladdin.

"She is inside your palace in Africa,"
replied the genie.

"How did the palace and the princess
get to Africa?" Aladdin asked in surprise.

"The magician ordered the Genie
of the Lamp to move them," said the genie.

"Can you bring them back to me?" Aladdin pleaded.

"I'm sorry master," replied the genie.
"Only the Genie of the Lamp can return them."

"Can you take me to the palace?" asked Aladdin.

"Of course, Master," replied the genie.

The genie carried Aladdin to the palace
in Africa. When they arrived,
Aladdin crept quietly into the palace.

The princess was overjoyed
to see Aladdin.

"You've come to rescue me!" she cried.

"Once I find the lamp, I can
take us home," replied Aladdin.

"The magician always keeps the lamp
in his pocket," she told him, looking worried.

Aladdin had an idea.

"When the magician returns," said Aladdin,
"Put this berry in his drink."

"What will it do to him?" asked
the princess.

"It will make him fall into a deep sleep,"
Aladdin replied.

Later that day, the magician
returned to the palace.

"Bring me something to eat and drink,"
he ordered the princess.

The princess placed the berry
in the magician's drink and gave it to him.

Soon, the magician grew tired.
He fell to the floor in a deep sleep.

"Come, Aladdin," said the princess. "The magician is asleep."

Aladdin picked up the lamp and called the genie.

"Carry us back home,"
he told the genie.

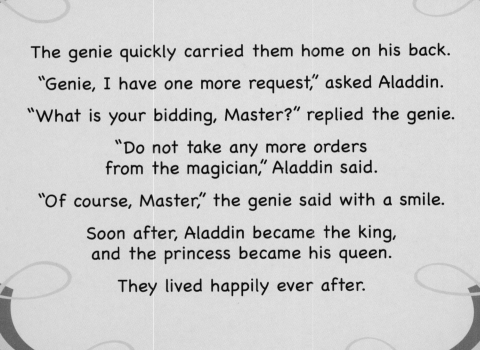

The genie quickly carried them home on his back.

"Genie, I have one more request," asked Aladdin.

"What is your bidding, Master?" replied the genie.

"Do not take any more orders
from the magician," Aladdin said.

"Of course, Master," the genie said with a smile.

Soon after, Aladdin became the king,
and the princess became his queen.

They lived happily ever after.

Antoine Galland was born in Rollot, France in 1646. He worked for the French embassy in Istanbul and traveled to Syria. At the embassy he learned about various Arabic, Turkish and Persian fairytales.

It is believed that Galland heard the story of Aladdin from a Syrian storyteller, from Aleppo. Gallard wrote the story in French and published it for the first time in a volume of *One Thousand and One Nights* in 1709. No earlier source has been traced for the tale of Aladdin.